BLU'S WILD JOURNEY

ADAPTED BY CHRISTA ROBERTS

HARPER

An Imprint of HarperCollins Publishers

Rio 2: Blu's Wild Journey

RIO 2 © 2014 Twentieth Century Fox Film Corporation.
All Rights Reserved.
Printed in China.
No part of this book may be used or reproduced in any manner
whatsoever without written permission except in the case of brief
quotations embodied in critical articles and reviews.
For information address HarperCollins Children's Books,
a division of HarperCollins Publishers,
10 East 53rd Street, New York, NY 10022.
www.harpercollinschildrens.com

This exclusive edition was printed for Kohl's Department Stores, Inc.
(for distribution on behalf of Kohl's Cares, LLC, its wholly owned subsidiary)
by HarperCollins Publishers.

Style #: 978-0-06-233480-0
Factory #: 123386
01/14

14 15 16 17 18 SCP 10 9 8 7 6 5 4 3 2 1

Not too long ago, Blu had thought he was the only blue Spix's Macaw left in the world. He lived in Minnesota with Linda, where she owned a bookstore. They didn't have many customers, but they had each other.

One day, a man came to the shop. "I've come six thousand miles looking for the two of you," he told Linda.

The man's name was Tulio. He studied birds, and his specialty was the rare blue Spix's Macaw. He wanted Blu and Linda to come to Brazil with him. "As far as we know, Blu is the last male of his kind," Tulio said. "We recently found a female of this kind. We hope to bring them together to save the species."

Linda and Blu went to Rio with Tulio. They were overwhelmed by the sights and sounds of the big city. It was Carnaval—the biggest party of the year.

But when Blu met Jewel, he forgot about everything else. She was the most beautiful bird he had ever seen.

Jewel didn't think much of Blu at first. He was a bird that couldn't fly, and she was a wild bird that wanted to escape from the aviary and find her way back home.

But the two became fast friends. They met other animals in Rio who helped them adjust to the city, too. And soon, Rio had become their home.

Now, Blu and Jewel and their three children—Carla, Bia, and Tiago—lived with Linda and Tulio at the sanctuary they had created in Rio. Life was good. And on New Year's Eve, as Blu sat with his family and watched the fireworks pop over the city, he wished that nothing would change.

At that same moment, Linda and Tulio were on an expedition deep in the Amazon rain forest. They were returning a baby bird they'd nurtured back to health to its home.

Suddenly, the river rapids swept them downstream and over a waterfall. When they surfaced at the bottom, they made their way to dry land to catch their breath. As they sat there, trying to figure out where they had landed, a bird zipped over their heads and one lone feather fell to the ground. A bright *blue* feather. Linda and Tulio looked at each other in awe. It belonged to a blue Spix's Macaw.

Back in Rio, Blu and the kids were busy making breakfast. *Flip!* A pancake sailed through the air. *Squirt!* Carla sprayed whipped cream on top.

Jewel flew in with a Brazil nut clutched in her beak. She couldn't believe the sight before her. She pulled Blu aside—she wanted him to help her show their kids how to be birds, not people.

But everything stopped when Tulio and Linda appeared on TV. Tulio showed the feather they'd found and announced that a flock of blue Spix's Macaws might be living in the jungle.

"We're not the only ones!" Jewel cried excitedly. "We have to get out to the wild and be birds, Blu!"

Carla, Bia, and Tiago cheered. An adventure into the wild sounded like a good idea to them, too. But Blu wasn't so sure.

Blu hurried to find his friends. He told Rafael, Nico, and Pedro that Jewel wanted to take the kids to the Amazon to look for more birds of their kind. He couldn't understand why she would want to change their situation when everything was going so well. But his friends convinced him it would be a good trip for the whole family—a vacation in the wild!

"If this is important to Jewel, just do it," Rafael said. "Happy wife, happy life."

It was a beautiful trip. The birds flew from Rio to Ouro Preto. They perched on top of a cathedral where they could see the entire city. Carla, Bia, and Tiago had never been anywhere outside of Rio. They couldn't get enough of the new sights.

The family flew for the rest of the day and into the night. The kids were growing weary. They were ready to get to the vacation portion of the trip!

Blu and Jewel gave the kids a lift. Carla, Bia, and Tiago slept soundly as their parents carried them through the night.

The family flew on. As they coasted over a river, they spotted an old riverboat steaming along. What luck! They swooped down to hitch a ride.

Blu and Jewel sat on top of the boat as it moved slowly down the river. The sun was beginning to set; it cast a pink-and-gold glow over the water.

Jewel spread her wings and let the wind ruffle her feathers. She was so happy to be out in the open air.

Blu was nervous to be going to such a wild place. He couldn't help but look back toward the city a few times as the boat moved farther down the river. But the sight of Jewel made him hopeful that this new adventure would be exciting.

"Thank you for doing this," Jewel said.

"I would do anything for you," Blu replied. And he meant it.

The birds remained on the old riverboat into the night.
It was nice to rest their wings for a little while.

At first light, the travelers were well rested. They flew off with high hopes and renewed excitement. Jewel felt so at home being back in the wild.

The birds finally landed in the jungle. They looked around, but there was no sign of Linda or Tulio. There was no sign of any other macaws.

Blu checked his GPS. He'd programmed in the exact coordinates of Linda and Tulio's camp. Could they have missed a turn? Or landed in the wrong part of the jungle?

Suddenly, a flash of blue caught Jewel's eye. Blu watched as she looked up into the tree canopy, then followed her gaze. Blu couldn't believe what they were seeing. . . .

Perched in the branches overhead were dozens of blue
Spix's Macaws!

"I can't believe we found them," Jewel said, breathless.

Blu had to admit it was an amazing sight. They'd come
so far from Rio, and here was the very thing they'd been
searching for—more of their kind!

"What is going on?" an angry voice boomed out of the shadows. A large bird appeared and looked down at the new arrivals. "Who are you? Where did you come from?"

Blu wasn't sure what to do. But Jewel walked up to the bird and gave him a little push. "Hey!" she said. "Back off!"

She stared into his eyes, then gasped. "I can't believe it," she said.

"How . . . how . . . is this?" the other bird said. "I've looked everywhere for you!"

Jewel couldn't believe her eyes. It was her father, Eduardo!

"My daughter has returned!" Eduardo said proudly. He hugged Jewel. Then he turned to meet his grandchildren.

Blu looked on from the background. This was the family Jewel had been taken from, and here they all were, tucked away in the Amazon. An entire tribe of blue Spix's Macaws!

Blu tried to join the happy reunion, but Eduardo was tough. He kept calling Blu "Stu." Blu hadn't felt as far from home as he did now, watching Jewel greet old family and friends.

Eduardo led the way to the macaws' village. Hidden behind a waterfall in a verdant, green forest were even *more* blue Spix's Macaws.

Blu couldn't believe how far he had come. He was once thought to be the only male blue Spix's Macaw left in the entire world. Now he had a beautiful wife, three amazing children, and an entire jungle full of birds just like him. They were no longer the last of their kind!

He knew there would be challenges to face and other birds to impress, but Blu was proud of himself. It had been a wild journey for the little blue Spix's Macaw from Minnesota. And now it was time to celebrate with new family and friends.

THE END